THIS BOOK BELONGS TO

361 00413 3

Published by Purnell Books, Paulton, Bristol,
BS18 5LQ, a member of the BPCC group of companies.
Reprinted 1983
Made and printed in Great Britain by Purnell and Sons
(Book Production) Ltd, Paulton, Bristol.

NODDY
AND TESSIE BEAR

BY
Enid Blyton

CONTENTS

LONDON
SAMPSON LOW, MARSTON & CO., LTD.
AND THE RICHARDS PRESS, LTD.

© 1961
by Enid Blyton
as to the text herein and
by Sampson Low, Marston & Co., Ltd.
as to the artwork herein

NODDY SANG AS HE WORKED, AND MR. TUBBY BEAR
CAME TO LISTEN

1. ONE WINDY MORNING

ONE morning, when Noddy opened his front
door, the wind rushed in and nearly blew
him over.

"Whooo-ooo-ooo!" said the wind at the top
of its voice, and blew some flowers out of a jug
on Noddy's table.

"Don't!" said Noddy. "Now look at the mess
you've made! It's my busy morning, too!"

He shut the front door and put the flowers
back into the vase. The wind jiggled at the door
as if it was trying to come in again.

"Aha—I'm going out of the *back* door this time, Wind!" said Noddy. "You're not going to rush at me again!"

So he went to the back door, opened it and slipped out. But, of course, the wind was waiting for him there, too, and blew his hat right off and over the wall into Mr. Tubby Bear's garden.

Noddy fetched it and put it very firmly on his head. "You can't blow it off now, Wind!" he said. "You can only jingle my bell, and I like you to do that!"

The wind blew again and the bell jingled loudly and merrily. "Jingle-jingle-jingle-jing!"

Noddy filled his pail with water, took his big sponge and his duster and polish, and went to clean his car. It had rained the day before, and the little car was dirty and splashed with mud. That would never do!

The wind blew hard all the time, and tugged at Noddy's yellow scarf and jingled his bell.

"You really seem as if you want to have a game with me, Wind," said Noddy, sponging the mud from his car. "You make me feel excited and happy. I think I'm going to sing a song, Wind—and it's about *you*!"

So he sang as he worked, and Mr. Tubby Bear came to listen, because it really was a gay little song.

> "Oh, Wind, you're very rough today,
>   You blow the clouds along,
>   You puff my chimney smoke away

9

And sing a windy song.
You shake the washing to and
   fro,
You make me dance and sing,
You take my little bell and blow
To make it jingle-jing!
   Jingle-jingle-jingle-jing!
   Oh, it is a happy thing
   To have a little bell to ring!"

And then Mr. Tubby Bear joined in and sang in his deep growly voice, too. "Jingle-jingle-jingle-jing! Oh, it is a happy thing! To have a little bell to ring!"

Noddy laughed, and his head nodded up and down very fast. "Oh, Mr. Tubby Bear, I didn't know you were listening!" he said. "*Isn't* the wind windy today!"

"Yes," said Mr. Tubby Bear, "and isn't the water wet! Really, it's very very wet today—you put your hand in your pail and feel!"

"I shan't!" said Noddy, laughing. "You're just having a joke with me. Oooh, Mr. Tubby— look, the wind has blown Mrs. Tubby's washing down—what *will* she say?" They ran to pick up the washing, and the wind tried its best to blow

it away before they could get to it. It blew Noddy's
hat off again—and, dear me, Mr. Tubby Bear picked
it up with the washing and pegged it on the line!

Noddy helped him to peg everything up.
"Here's your new vest," he said. "And here are
two socks—ooh, this one's got such a big hole
in, Mr. Tubby! And here's your red hanky—it's
so big I could almost use it for a table-cloth!"

Soon they had pegged up everything and Noddy
went off happily to polish his car again. He didn't
know that his hat was pegged up on the line in
Mr. Tubby's garden!

"Listen, car," said Noddy. "I'll sing you my
new windy song again."

2. A DEAR LITTLE VISITOR

NODDY began to sing his song very loudly, and when he came to the jingle-jingle bit he nodded his head to make his bell ring. But it didn't. There was no sound at all.

"Why don't you ring?" said Noddy, surprised, and stood there nodding his head again and again and again to make his bell go jingle-jing.

Now little Tessie Bear was just passing by at that moment, and she was *most* surprised to see Noddy standing all by himself in his front garden, nodding and nodding and nodding.

"Good morning, little Noddy!" she called. "Why are you standing there, nodding at nothing?"

"Oh—it's little Tessie Bear," said Noddy, very pleased. "Hallo!" He nodded his head very fast at her, but still his bell didn't ring.

"I'm trying to make the bell on my hat ring, but it won't," said Noddy, sadly.

"But you haven't got your hat on," said Tessie Bear, still surprised.

"Haven't I?" said Noddy, puzzled, and put his hand up to his head. "Dear me—where's it gone? Oh, the wind must have been playing tricks with me again—it's blown it away. Wherever can it be?"

Tessie Bear gave a little giggle. "*I* know where it is," she said. "It's pegged up on the line in Mr. Tubby Bear's garden—look!"

"*Well!*" said Noddy, in surprise. "Fancy that!

The wind must have taken it off my head and pegged it up on the washing line! Whoever would have thought it could do *that*!"

"I'll fetch it for you," said Tessie Bear, and she put down her basket and ran into the Tubby Bears' garden. She unpegged the

13

little blue hat and took it
back to Noddy.

"There!" she said, and
she put it on his head.

"Jingle-jingle-jing," said
the little bell on the top.

"You *are* kind!" said
Noddy, pleased. "Shall I
sing you my windy song, Tessie? I only made it
up just now."

"Yes, do," said Tessie, so Noddy sang it at
the top of his voice while she listened.

"It's very very good," said Tessie, "especially
the jingle-jing bit. Your bell joined in nicely—
did you hear it?"

"Yes," said Noddy, beaming at her. "Tessie,
you've got a new bonnet. I do like it. It's got
red poppies in."

Tessie nodded and the poppies bobbed about.
She smiled at Noddy, and then she picked up her
basket to go. "I'm going to the market to sell
these eggs," she said.

"I'll take you in my car," said Noddy at
once, and the car gave a little jump and said
"Parp-parp" in a very pleased voice. It liked
little Tessie Bear.

"Oh no, Noddy—I haven't got sixpence to pay you for the ride," said Tessie Bear. "Look—I've only got one penny in my purse!"

"I wouldn't let *you* pay me," said Noddy. "I'm doing it because I do so like the poppies in your bonnet. It will be nice to see them bobbing beside me in the car."

"Well, I'll let you take me if you'll take one of my eggs and not pay for it," said Tessie. "See—here is the biggest and the brownest—I'll give you that, and you must have it for your breakfast."

"Oh—*thank* you! " said Noddy, nodding his head at top speed. " I do think you are the kindest little bear I've ever met."

He took the egg carefully into his house, and then he put Tessie and her basket into his car and away they went.

Tessie Bear had hardly ever had a ride in a car, and she really did enjoy it. She held her basket of eggs very carefully on her plump little lap, afraid of breaking them.

"Parp-parp!" said the car, importantly, as they went carefully down the street. It wanted everyone to see what a dear little passenger it had that morning.

Noddy didn't bump into any lamp-posts, and when he saw Sally Skittle's mischievous little children playing in the road he didn't knock them down as they hoped he would but stopped until they were out of the way.

"Skittles like to be knocked down," he told

Tessie Bear, "but you make me feel very kind, Tessie, so I don't even *want* to knock them over."

Mr. Plod was standing at the corner, and he was most astonished to see Noddy being so polite to the skittles.

"Good morning, Mr. Plod; we're off to the market," said Noddy, glad

16

THE SAILOR DOLL SANG A VERY LOUD AND
ROLLICKING SONG

that Mr. Plod had seen him driving so carefully.

"PARP!" hooted the car, suddenly, and made Mr. Plod jump. It didn't like Mr. Plod.

"Look, Noddy—there's a sailor doll beckoning to you," said Tessie. "He wants to hire your car. I'd better get out and let him get in. You mustn't lose a sixpenny fare because of me."

"No, no, don't you get out!" said Noddy at once. "The sailor doll can sit in the back."

So he stopped and the sailor got in, singing a very loud and rollicking song.

> "Yo-ho, yo-ho!
> Now off you go
> To the third little house
> In Rimminy Row!"

"I'm on my way to market, so I'll drop you at Rimminy Row as I pass," said Noddy.

"YO-HO, YO-HO . . ." began the sailor again, and made Noddy jump. The car swerved and almost knocked a tree over.

"Don't sing your song so near my ear," said Noddy. So the sailor sang it quietly, and it was such a funny little song that Tessie Bear and Noddy soon joined in, and away they went down the street singing merrily.

"Yo-ho, yo-ho!
  Now off we go
  To the third little house
  In Rimminy Row! "

"Here we are," said Noddy, as the car drew up at a tiny house that really looked more like a boat than a house. "Sixpence, please."

"Here's a shilling," said the sailor doll, who seemed a very merry fellow. "Yo-ho, yo-ho, now in I go, back to my house in Rimminy Row!"

"He's rather nice, isn't he?" said Noddy to Tessie Bear. "Now we're almost at the market. I do hope you sell your eggs, Tessie. Look at my shilling—I'll buy something *nice* with that!"

3. THE LOVELY KITE

TESSIE went to stand at a corner of the market, and the red poppies in her hat were so gay that everyone looked at the little bear. They came to buy her eggs and soon her basket was quite empty.

Noddy was still in the market, looking all round for something to buy with his shilling—something for little Tessie Bear. He simply could NOT make up his mind what to get.

"A red necklace to match the poppies in her hat? No—that nice one is more than a shilling. What about this little bow to wear under her chin? But perhaps she has one at home like that. "Oh dear!" said Noddy. "I really think

I had better ask Tessie herself what she would like."

Tessie was looking at a market stall with gay scarves hanging over it. Noddy went to her.

"Tessie—do you want one of those scarves?" he said. "I'll buy you one—a red one to match the poppies!"

"Oh no, Noddy," said Tessie Bear. "I was just thinking I would buy *you* a scarf. See— what about this blue one?"

"But I'm wearing a scarf already. Haven't you noticed?" said Noddy. "Tessie, do come round the market with me and choose something for me to buy for *you.*"

"I don't know *any*thing I want," said Tessie, patting Noddy with her soft little paw. "But

let's walk round and see if we can find something nice."

So they walked off together, and the wind blew Tessie's poppies up and down and made Noddy's bell go jingle-jing all the time.

They came to the kite-stall, and the Wobbly-Woman behind it called out to them.

"Kites for sale, kites for sale.
See them fly
Far on high,
Up to the clouds in the windy sky,
Each with a wriggly, jiggly tail.
Kites for sale, KITES FOR SALE!"

One kite flapped and shivered and wriggled on the stall as it tried to get away on the wind that swooped all round.

"Ooooh, Noddy!" said Tessie Bear, stopping suddenly. "Look at that kite! Could we buy it, do you think—it does so want to have a game in

the windy sky! Is it too much money?" "It's one shilling and sixpence," said the fat little Wobbly-Woman behind the stall. She wobbled round to them with the flapping kite. "See what a beauty it is—strong

22

as the wind. It will fly higher than any kite before!"

"Noddy—we've got one and sixpence between us," said Tessie. "Oh, Noddy—would it be a waste of money to spend it on a kite?"

"We'll have it!" said Noddy "I like it, too. Kite, we'll buy you, and you shall fly in the sky for us, and we will hold you tight!"

So they paid the Wobbly-Woman the one and sixpence and took the kite away. It was very big, and Tessie and Noddy had to hold on to it very tightly. The wind caught sight of it and rushed down—and, dear me, it blew the kite so hard that it made Noddy and Tessie run very fast.

"Where shall we fly it?" asked Noddy.

"Let's go up to the farm," said Tessie, excited. "It's a good way off, but we could go in your car, couldn't we?"

"Yes, if you could somehow manage to hold the kite," said Noddy. "Perhaps you could sit on the back, Tessie, and hold it tight. Don't get blown off, whatever you do."

Well, off they went in the car, with Tessie holding as tightly as she could to the flapping kite. *How* it tried to get away! In the end Noddy had to drive with one hand and hold on to Tessie with the other.

At last they came to the farm. The farmer was there, with a big churn full of milk. He set it beside the lane so that the milkman could pick it up and take it away to sell. He called to Noddy, "Now then, Noddy, what do you and Tessie want?"

"We wondered if you'd let us fly our lovely big kite in your field, Mr. Straw," said Noddy, holding the kite tightly.

"Yes—if you and Tessie will do something for me first," said the farmer. "I want the eggs taken out of my hen-house and put into this basket. Then put the basket on top of the churn for the milkman to collect with the milk."

"Oh—we'd *like* to do that," said Noddy, pleased. "At least—I'll have to hold the kite. Can you get them, Tessie?"

"Oh yes," said the little bear. "I'm used to collecting eggs from my own hens."

So, while Noddy tied some string to the end of the kite and shook out its tail, Tessie took the basket and went to get the eggs.

"I won't be long!" she called, and opened the gate of the hen-run to go to the hen-house. "Shoo, shoo! I haven't come to feed you, I've come for your eggs. SHOO!"

4. FLY, KITE, FLY!

NODDY had the kite all ready to fly when Tessie came out of the hen-run with the basket full of eggs.

"I'll just put the basket on top of the churn," called Tessie. "There were such a lot of eggs!"

She set the basket carefully on the churn and then ran to Noddy.

"We'll *both* have to hold this kite when it flies up into the air," said Noddy. "It does pull so hard. It's longing to fly. Now—I'll let out the string, Tessie—oooh, do be careful!"

Whooooosh! Away went the big kite with a rush into the air, its tail dancing behind it.

FLY, KITE, FLY!

"There it goes!" cried Noddy. "Fly, kite, fly, high up in the sky, come down by-and-by, fly, kite, fly!"

The string ran quickly through his fingers, and when he held it tight to stop the kite's flight for a second Tessie had to hold the string, too. Oh, what fun it was!

"It's going up to the clouds!" said Noddy, nodding his head till his bell jingled a gay little tune. "Look out, kite, you'll bump your head—oh, it's gone right through that cloud, Tessie, and made a hole in it."

At last there was no more string left—the kite had used it all up. "Hold tight, now, Tessie, hold tight!" said Noddy in alarm, because the

kite was pulling so very very hard. "Oh, it's pulling me along!"

"Let's sit down and hold it," said Tessie. "It can't make us run along then! Sit down, Noddy, quickly!"

So they both sat down and then it was easier to hold the kite. They sang together.

> "Fly, kite, fly,
>   High up in the sky,
>   Come down by-and-by,
>   Fly, kite, fly!"

At the end of the song Tessie suddenly gave a little jump and said, "Ooooh!"

"What's the matter?" asked Noddy in surprise.

"Something's pecking the poppies in my

28

bonnet," said Tessie. "Oooh! What is it?"

"A hen—a big white hen!" said Noddy. "Shoo, hen! How dare you!"

And then, dear me, another hen came up and pecked at Noddy's shoe-laces. "Don't!" said Noddy, crossly. "DON'T DO THAT, hen—they're shoe-laces, not worms."

"Where did these hens come from?" said Tessie, puzzled. "There were none round us just now. Oh, do stop, hen—you'll *spoil* my new bonnet!"

And then Noddy looked at Tessie in such alarm that she felt quite scared. "What's the matter, Noddy?" she said. "Why are you looking at me like that?"

29

"Oh, *Tessie*!" said Noddy. "You left the gate of the hen-run open! You forgot to shut it when you went for the eggs—and ALL the hens are out!"

Tessie gave a squeal. "What will the farmer say? Oh, Noddy, he'll be so cross with me."

"We'll have to shoo all the hens back," said Noddy. "Oh, do stop pecking my laces, hen. Don't you know what a *real* worm looks like?"

30

"But, Noddy, we can't hold the kite-string and shoo the hens as well," said Tessie. "You know we can't. And even if you hold the string by yourself I'll never be able to shoo so many hens—look, there are dozens running about loose."

"Never mind, little Tessie Bear," said Noddy, nodding kindly at her. "I'll tell you what we can do. We'll tie the string to something, and then the kite will be quite safe and won't be able to fly away. Then we'll both shoo the hens!"

"Noddy, you are very very clever," said Tessie, looking at him with such big round eyes that Noddy felt very proud indeed. "What shall we tie the string to?"

"Well—what's nearest?" said Noddy. "Look— that heavy churn of milk! We could tie the string to its big handle, and then the kite would be held safely. We'll run to the churn, Tessie. Come on!"

Off they ran together with the string, and soon Noddy had tied it very tightly indeed to the handle of the big churn. "Now we'll chase those peckity hens!" said Noddy.

31

5. A HORRID SHOCK

TESSIE BEAR and Noddy chased the hens all over the field. They were very naughty hens and not one of them would go into the hen-run.

"I know, Noddy," panted Tessie at last. "Go to the hen-run gate and take off your hat. Jingle the bell and the hens will all come to see what the noise is—and you'll be able to shoo them inside."

"Now *you're* very very clever, Tessie," said Noddy, and he did exactly as she had told him. Jingle-jingle went his little bell as he stood by the hen-run gate and shook his blue hat. All the hens heard it and wanted to know what it was. They scampered over the field to the gate, and Noddy shooed them all in very quickly. He shut the gate and then smiled at Tessie.

"Now we'll go back to our kite," he said. But, goodness me, when they went towards the churn they had a dreadful shock! Whatever do you think was happening?

The kite was pulling so hard that the churn was wobbling—then it gave a little jump—and then away it went into the air, swinging to and fro at the end of the string! What a sight to see!

Noddy shouted, "Stop, churn, stop! Come down again! How dare you—you've got that basket of eggs, too. Kite, come down at once and bring the churn!"

33

But the kite and the churn took no notice of Noddy at all. The kite flew higher still, and the churn followed, swaying to and fro. Noddy felt dreadful. He turned to speak to Tessie Bear and then he felt more dreadful still. The little bear was crying big tears down her furry nose! "The farmer will spank me for letting his hens out—and he'll spank you too," wept Tessie.

"I won't *let* him spank you," said Noddy, bravely. "I'll tell him to give *me* two spankings instead. Shut your eyes, Tessie, and I'll rub the tears off your nose."

"No, no—we mustn't lose any time!" said Tessie, pushing Noddy's hand away from her nose. "We must get into your car and follow the churn—we can easily see it flying through the air. We'll watch where it comes down and then take it back to the farmer."

"The eggs will all be broken," said Noddy, gloomily. "This is a most terrible thing to happen. Come on, then—let's get into my car."

They both went sadly to the little car and got into it. "Parp!" said the car in surprise when some of Tessie's tears splashed on its bonnet. But Noddy didn't even rub them off—he drove quickly over the field after the kite and the churn. Oh dear, oh dear—would he ever catch them up?

Hurry, Noddy, hurry—and be careful of that little pond—there, you nearly went into it. Keep your eyes in front and not up in the air—oh, hurry, Noddy, hurry.

6. A MOST PECULIAR THING

NOW just as Noddy and Tessie Bear had set off in the little car, Big-Ears, Noddy's friend, came riding into Toy Village on his bicycle. He saw Miss Fluffy Cat and Mr. Toy Dog and stopped to talk to them.

And it was exactly at that moment that a MOST peculiar thing happened. A big brown egg fell out of the air right on to Mr. Toy Dog's head! It broke at once, and there was **Mr. Toy Dog** looking surprised and angry, with yellow egg-yolk dripping down his neck!

"Who did that?" said **Mr. Toy Dog**, angrily, looking all round. "Who threw that egg at me?"

"Somebody round the corner, perhaps," said Big-Ears, surprised, too. "That naughty Gilbert Golly, I expect—or, perhaps, Bruiny Bear—he's not been very well-behaved lately."

They went to look—and then another peculiar thing happened. It began to rain out of a clear blue sky! How very extraordinary!

Miss Fluffy Cat stared at the drops that fell on her sleeve. They were white! She licked them and then said a most surprising thing.

"It's raining milk! It's actually raining MILK!"

37

"Nonsense!" said Big-Ears. "It never rains milk. I'm about a hundred years old and I've *never* known it rain milk."

"Big-Ears, *I* ought to know milk when I taste it!" said Miss Fluffy Cat, quite crossly. "I've lived on it all my life—and I tell you it's raining *milk*."

"I'm going to get an umbrella," said Mr. Toy Dog, hurrying off. "If it's raining milk it may rain gravy next, or treacle—and I'm not going to have my new suit spoilt."

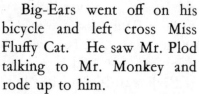

Big-Ears went off on his bicycle and left cross Miss Fluffy Cat. He saw Mr. Plod talking to Mr. Monkey and rode up to him.

"Mr. Plod—it's raining milk!" he said. "And just now an egg fell on Mr. Toy Dog's head."

"Don't be so silly, Big-Ears!" said Mr. Plod—and then, will you believe it, just at that *very* moment an egg fell out of the air right on to Mr. Plod's big right boot.

SPLASH!

The yellow yolk flew all round and Mr. Monkey was splashed on his legs.

"There—what did I tell you!" said Big-Ears. "Raining milk and eggs! See—there's another shower of milk falling. We ought to get our jugs and fill them."

A golliwog came hurrying up with Mr. Noah and Sally Skittle. The golliwog looked very funny because he had an egg all over his black hair.

"Mr. Plod! The Ark's been hit by three eggs!" shouted Mr. Noah.

"And my smallest skittle was knocked over by one!" said Sally Skittle. "And we are all *drenched* with milk. Whatever is happening?"

Nobody could *think* what was going on—and everyone in Toy Village felt very frightened. They looked up into the sky, but all they could see was a kite very high up and something that glittered a little now and again. That was the milk-churn still hanging on the end of the string, of course, but it was much too far away to see exactly what it was.

"Sound the fire-bell, Mr. Plod," begged Mr. Noah. "Get everyone under cover. You don't know what's going to rain on us next—bricks, maybe—sticks, stones—why, there must be enemies about."

"This is all very strange," said Mr. Plod. "I will put up a notice and offer a LARGE reward to anyone who can tell us what is happening. Get under cover, now!"

Mr. Plod went into the police-station, just escaping another egg, and wrote out a very large notice, which he pinned up outside the police-station.

MR. PLOD PINNED UP A VERY LARGE NOTICE
OUTSIDE THE POLICE-STATION

41

REWARD!

A LARGE reward of FIVE GOLDEN POUNDS offered to anyone giving information about the RAIN OF MILK and EGGS. This is VERY URGENT and IMPORTANT.

But nobody came to tell him anything, and all Toy Village was most alarmed and very puzzled. Whatever would happen next? Eggs and milk were bad enough—but soon there might be much worse things!

"I must go and see if Noddy is safely in his house," thought Big-Ears, and he set off on his bicycle at top speed. "He really must be feeling very frightened."

7. A CHASE AFTER THE KITE

BUT Noddy was not in his little House-For-One, of course. Big-Ears bicycled back to the police-station, feeling very worried. He arrived just as Mr. Straw the farmer rode up on his old horse.

"Mr. Plod, Mr. Plod!" bellowed the farmer. "Where are you? I've come to tell you that someone has stolen my milk-churn and all my eggs."

"Well! What a day this is!" said Mr. Plod, taking his pencil out and beginning to write in his notebook. "Er—a *milk*-churn, did you say—and eggs? Good gracious—did you know it had been raining eggs and milk in the village? Would it be anything to do with *your* milk and eggs?"

"Are you being funny, Mr. Plod?" asked Mr. Straw, astonished. "Whoever heard of milk and egg rain! Don't you make fun of *me*, Mr. Plod, or I'll report you! As if I'd rain milk and eggs on this village from my churn!"

"I didn't mean that, Mr. Straw," said Mr. Plod. "I just meant it was funny that you'd missed a milk-churn and eggs, and those are just the things that have been falling out of the sky on us this morning. Look at my right boot—all splashed with egg!"

"If you're trying to say that *I* threw an egg at you . . ." began the angry farmer, and then he stopped. An egg had just fallen on the window-sill and the pane was suddenly splashed with yellow.

"There you are!" said Mr. Plod. "See what I mean? It's very strange, and I've offered a LARGE reward to anyone who can tell me the meaning of all this. The toys are very frightened, Mr. Straw—and we don't know what may happen next."

44

"Well—if those are *my* eggs and milk someone is throwing about, I'd like to know who it is!" said the farmer. "Here, *I'll* give a reward, too, Mr. Plod—ten shillings to anyone bringing back my milk-churn. It's the only one I've got. Put up a notice!"

So Mr. Plod wrote another notice and pinned it up beside his first one. Mr. Straw got on his horse and set off home, looking out for any eggs falling unexpectedly from above.

"It's very, very strange," said Mr. Plod to Big-Ears. "I don't like it."

"Nor do I," said Big-Ears. "And I'm worried about little Noddy, too—he *should* be back

home now after his morning's work, but he's not. I think I'll stay with you for a while and see if you get any news about anything."

"I wonder who stole the milk-churn and where it is now," said Mr. Plod.

Well, the milk-churn wasn't up in the sky any longer. The string had broken and the churn had fallen down and down—and landed BUMP in the middle of a thick bush.

The kite flew right away in the air as soon as it felt itself free, and made up its mind to reach the big shining sun. It hadn't liked the big heavy churn pulling it downwards all the time. The egg basket had fallen down a long while back and had bounced into some bracken.

Noddy and Tessie Bear had raced after the kite as fast as they could. Tessie gave a little cry when she saw the basket fall.

"We can pick that up," she said. "Oh, Noddy —the kite must have flown right over Toy Village.

46

Suppose the eggs fell there!—Whatever would people think?"

"I can't imagine," said Noddy, as the car bumped down a rough lane. "Look, Tessie— there's the basket, over in that clump of bracken by the wayside. At least we can take *that* back to the farmer."

On they went, and Tessie kept her eye on the swinging milk-churn high up in the sky. "It's spilling milk all the time," she said. "Will it rain on anyone, do you think?"

"Goodness—I hope not!" said Noddy, driving fast. "We'll get into enough trouble without that!"

"Noddy, Noddy—the churn's falling down, it's falling!" suddenly cried Tessie Bear, and she

clutched so hard at Noddy that the car nearly
went into a stream. "The string must have
broken. Oh, we'll be able to get the churn!"

They came to the churn at last. There it lay,
in the middle of a bush, almost empty now, for
its lid had long ago fallen off. Noddy stopped
his car and got out. Tessie got out, too, and
together they dragged the churn into the car.

Noddy stood it at the back and tied a rope
round it. He gave the ends to Tessie. "Now
you hold on tightly to those," he said, "and
then the churn will keep steady."

"What are we going to do, Noddy?" said Tessie, trying to be brave.

"I'm going to drive through Toy Village and then on to Mr. Straw's farm," said Noddy. "I expect he will do a bit of spanking, Tessie, so you'd better not come right to the farmhouse."

"I don't want you to be spanked, Noddy," said Tessie Bear, the tears running down her furry nose again. "You're so nice and I do like you so much."

"Do you?" said Noddy, in surprise. "Oh, I *am* glad. But don't you worry about me, little Tessie Bear—or yourself either. I won't let *anyone* be unkind to you. If they are, I'll—I'll—well, I haven't quite made up my mind *what* I'll do."

49

"Shall we get into a *lot* of trouble?" asked Tessie, the poppies in her hat bobbing as the car went jolting along.

"I expect *I* shall, because of the churn," said Noddy. "And I'll have to pay for the milk and the eggs. But I can save up for those."

"I'll save up, too," said Tessie. "I'll get my hens to lay lots and lots of eggs and I'll sell them and give you all the money."

"You're a very, very good friend, Tessie," said Noddy, gratefully. "I've got Big-Ears for one good friend—and now I've got you, too, Tessie."

"Here's Toy Village," said Tessie. "Oooh, look—isn't that Big-Ears' bicycle outside the police-station?"

8. AT MR. PLOD'S

YES, it *was* Big-Ears' bicycle. Just as Noddy's little car came by, Big-Ears popped out to make sure that his bicycle was all right, and he suddenly saw little Noddy in his car with Tessie —and the big milk-churn!

He was *most* astonished. He ran in front of the car, shouting, "Noddy, Noddy, stop! Where have you been?"

Noddy almost drove into Big-Ears. He stopped his car so suddenly that the milk-churn fell off the back and rolled down the street with a most tremendous clanging noise. Mr. Plod came out of his police-station at a run.

"Hey! That's the missing milk-churn!" he shouted. "Why, Noddy—did *you* find it? What a bit of luck!"

"Noddy, come and tell us where you got the churn," said Big-Ears, "and you, too, Tessie Bear."

"No. No, I don't want to talk to Mr. Plod," said Noddy. "I know he will be angry with me."

"But you *must*," said Big-Ears, pointing to the big notice Mr. Plod had put up. "Look—

there's a ten-shilling reward for anyone who brings back the milk-churn."

"Good gracious!" said Noddy, surprised.

"And do you know anything about a curious rain of milk we've had?" asked Big-Ears. "And falling eggs, too—one fell on Mr. Toy Dog's head!"

Tessie gave a sudden little giggle, and Noddy laughed, too. "Well—yes, I suppose we do know something about milk and eggs falling out of the sky," said Noddy. "Is there *really* a reward for that?"

"Oh yes. Five whole pounds!" said Big-Ears. "You see, everyone was very, very frightened,

and Mr. Plod thought it was his duty to clear up the matter, and offer a reward to anyone who could explain what was happening. So you *must* come in and tell us all about it."

"I'll just pick up the milk-churn," said Noddy, suddenly beginning to feel very excited. Why—things might come right without a spanking after all!

Soon they were all in the police-station, and Mr. Plod looked at Noddy and Tessie importantly. He opened his notebook and licked the point of his pencil.

9. EVERYTHING IS ALL RIGHT!

"WELL," said Noddy, "Tessie and I bought a kite, and we took it to the farmer's field to try it."

"And I left the gate of the hen-run open and all the hens came out," said Tessie.

"So we tied the kite string to the farmer's milk-churn nearby and went to chase the hens back," went on Noddy. "And the kite pulled so hard on its string that it lifted the churn up into the air. . . ."

"And a basket of eggs on top of it," said Tessie.

"And there they were, up in the air at the end of our kite string," finished Noddy. "So I suppose *that's* how you had a rain of milk

and eggs—the milk spilt out of the churn and the eggs fell out of the basket.".

"Well I never!" said Mr. Plod, amazed. Noddy looked anxiously to see what Big-Ears thought of his story, and was quite alarmed to see his face going redder and redder. Was he very angry?

No, he wasn't. He was trying not to laugh—but it was no good, he *had* to! "Ho ho ho!" he roared. "HO HO HO! Oh, HO HO HO HO HO!"

That set Mr. Plod off, too, and he laughed till he fell off his chair and rolled on the floor. Noddy and Tessie were most astonished. "What are you laughing at, Mr. Plod?" asked Noddy.

"I'm laughing at the thought of the milk spilling down on us—and the eggs going plop-plop-plop everywhere," said Mr. Plod, wiping his eyes. "I never heard of such a thing in my life. Never! What are *you* laughing at, Big-Ears?"

"Oh, HO HO HO!" roared Big-Ears. "*I'm* laughing because you've got to hand out a large reward to these two little rascals here who flew

MR. PLOD LAUGHED TILL HE FELL OFF HIS CHAIR
AND ROLLED ON THE FLOOR

a kite and sent a most peculiar rain over the village—and Farmer Straw has got to hand them ten shillings for his churn. Oh, HO HO HO!"

"We won't take your five pounds, Mr. Plod," said Noddy, seeing that the policeman had stopped laughing as soon as he heard what Big-Ears said. "And of course we wouldn't *dream* of taking the farmer's ten shillings. We were going to save up to pay for the lost milk and eggs."

"What you *really* deserve is a spanking," said Mr. Plod, sternly. "All right, don't look so scared, I'm not going to give you one. I can see that it was all an accident. Now look here—I'll give you the five pounds, but you mustn't take the farmer's reward . . ."

"Oh, we *wouldn't*," said Tessie.

"And you must pay him out of the five pounds for his lost milk and eggs," said Mr. Plod. "Oh dear, oh dear—when I think of that egg falling plop on to Mr. Toy Dog's head, I—HO HO HO HO HO—I simply can't help laughing."

Tessie laughed, too, and took Noddy's hand. "It's all come right," she said, and the poppies bobbed about in her little bonnet. "Nobody's cross with us after all. And we'll have some money to spend, Noddy—fancy that!"

"I'm going to spend some now," said Noddy, standing up, his head nodding and his bell jingling. "Mr. Plod—Big-Ears—Tessie—you're all to come with me to the ice-cream shop and I'll order the biggest and the best ice-creams they have. Two for each of us. No—*three*! We'll take the milk-churn back afterwards."

So out they all went, and the wind at once rushed down at them and took off Mr. Plod's helmet and rolled it down the street at top speed. Tessie remembered Noddy's wind-song.

"Sing it again," she said.

So Noddy sang at the top of his voice as they all marched off to the ice-cream shop together.

"Oh, wind, you're very rough today,
    You blow the clouds along;
    You took our lovely kite away
    And that was very wrong.
    You flew the milk-churn in the air,
    And spilt it on the town,

And how you made the people stare
When eggs came falling down.
Oh, ho-ho-ho, oh, ho-ho-ho,
You make me dance and sing;
You take my little bell and blow
To make it jingle-jing!
Jingle-jingle-jingle-jing!
Oh, it is a happy thing
To have a little bell to ring!"

"That's a lovely song, Noddy," said Big-Ears. "I do like the ho-ho-ho part."

"And I like the jingle-jing," said little Tessie Bear.

"*Do* you?" said Noddy, pleased—and you should have heard his bell ringing then—jingle-jingle-jingle-jing-jing-jing . . . yes, I can hear it ringing even now!